Stories from Bug Garden

LISA MOSER

illustrated by GWEN MILLWARD

CANDLEWICK PRESS

THE GARDEN

The garden was old

and forgotten,

with a tumbledown wall

and a one-wheeled barrow.

No one came down the weedy path

to take care of it

or sit among the flowers.

So they moved in

one

by one

by one.

LADYBUG

Ladybug never liked her name.

A lady had to sip tea,

fold her napkin,

and sit up very tall.

But when no one was looking,

Ladybug ran barefoot,

made mud angels,

and whistled through a blade of grass.

HORSEFLY AND BUTTERFLY

"What are you doing?" asked Butterfly.

"I am running," said Horsefly.

"See the wind ripple my mane?

See my mighty hooves flash?

See my tail streaming behind?"

"No," said Butterfly.

"I don't see any of those things."

"Look again," said Horsefly

as he ran around the garden.

Butterfly watched closely.

"You know you're not a horse.

You're a horsefly.

A teeny, tiny bug."

Horsefly stopped running.

He looked at Butterfly and sniffed.

"Well, you're not butter, either."

Then he ran some more.

DRAGONFLY

"Halt!" said Dragonfly. "Go no farther."

Everyone went another way

except Horsefly.

"Go no farther," said Dragonfly.

"What will you do?" asked Horsefly.

"Will you breathe fire?"

"I don't do that," said Dragonfly.

"Will you scratch me with your dragon

claws?"

"Of course not," said Dragonfly.

"Then stand back," said Horsefly.

SMACK!

Right into a gob of tree sap.

"I told you not to go farther," said Dragonfly.

"I should have listened," said Horsefly.

JUST BEE

Bee sat on a lilac branch

and watched the clouds.

"Shouldn't you fly around?" asked Dragonfly.

"Shouldn't you sip nectar from flowers?" asked Lightning Bug.

"Shouldn't you make honey?" asked Horsefly.

"I don't want to do any of those things," said Bee.

"What do you want to do, then?"

Bee settled back to watch the clouds.

"Just be," said Bee.

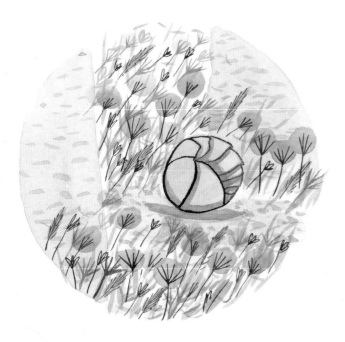

ROLY-POLY

Butterfly watched.

Roly-Poly curled up in a ball and started rolling.

"Wa-hoo!" said Roly-Poly.

He rolled past the peach trees.

"Wa-hoo!"

He rolled out the gate.

"Wa-hoo!"

He rolled down the path.

"Wa-hoo!"

Then he unrolled and started back.

"It's a long walk," said Butterfly.

"Yes, it is," huffed Roly-Poly.

"It will take hours and hours," said Butterfly.

"Maybe even longer," puffed Roly-Poly.

"You'll be tired when you get there," said Butterfly.

"Very, very, very tired," said Roly-Poly.

"What will you do when you get back?" asked Butterfly.

Roly-Poly looked at him and grinned.

"I'm going to do it all over again."

BIG ANT AND LITTLE ANT

One hot summer day,

the bugs had barely finished their picnic

when Roly-Poly called, "Hurry! Hurry! It's about to start."

Big Ant and Little Ant followed everyone and picked a spot.

"Look up," said Big Ant. "The big show will be up there."

"What will I see?" asked Little Ant.

"You'll see all sorts of colors: red, pink, blue, yellow, orange . . ."

said Big Ant. "They'll come in every shape and size, too."

Little Ant snuggled closer to Big Ant. . . .

POP!

"Ooohhh!" cheered the bugs.

BOOM!

"Aaahhh!" cheered the bugs.

Little Ant and Big Ant watched the colors dance and swirl up above.

"That was the most beautiful thing I ever saw," said Little Ant.

"Yes," agreed Big Ant. "It's always a spectacular show when the flowers bloom."

CRICKET

A strong wind frisked and frolicked among the flowers.
Cricket hurried and hopped onto the gate.
Whoosh! The gate creaked from its resting place
and swung forward.

"Farewell. Farewell. I am leaving on a grand
adventure. I don't know if I will ever see you
again," called Cricket.

Whoosh! The gate swung back.
"I was wrong. I am back. I will never
leave again."

Whoosh! The gate swung forward.
"I'm off! I'm off to do
marvelous deeds...."

Whoosh! The gate swung back.
"My mistake. So sorry."

Whoosh! The gate swung forward.
"Good-bye, dear friends. I am the greatest
cricket explorer in the world...."

Bee turned to look at Snail. "How long will this go on?"

"Not much longer," said Snail. "Does everyone remember their jobs?"

"I'll latch the gate," said Ladybug.

"I'll wave and cheer," said Roly-Poly.

"And I'll get the sign," said Little Ant.

welcome home!

REACH A PEACH

Big Ant and Cricket looked at the pretty peach.

"The best way to reach a peach is at the top of the hop," said Cricket.

He jumped and jumped and jumped.

He tried to reach the peach.

"No," said Big Ant. "The best way to reach a peach is at the bottom of the drop."

She climbed up the tree and stood on the peach.

She jumped and jumped and jumped.

"Top of the hop," said Cricket, jumping.

"Bottom of the drop," said Big Ant, jumping.

"Top!"

"Drop!"

"Top!"

"Drop!"

"STOP!" said Big Ant. "We're never going to get this peach."

Cricket and Big Ant sat under the peach tree. A strong wind bopped through the garden.

KER-PLOP!

"Ah," said Cricket. "Now we know the very best way to reach a peach."

"Let the wind blow it down," said Big Ant.

CHOMP! CHOMP! CHOMP!

EARTHWORM

Bee loved the flowers best from way up high.

He buzzed among the bright petals.

Snail loved the flowers best from the ground.

She glided through the green jungle of stems.

But Earthworm loved the flowers best from way

down below.

She wiggled

　　and wiggled

　　　　and giggled

under the rainbows

of roots.

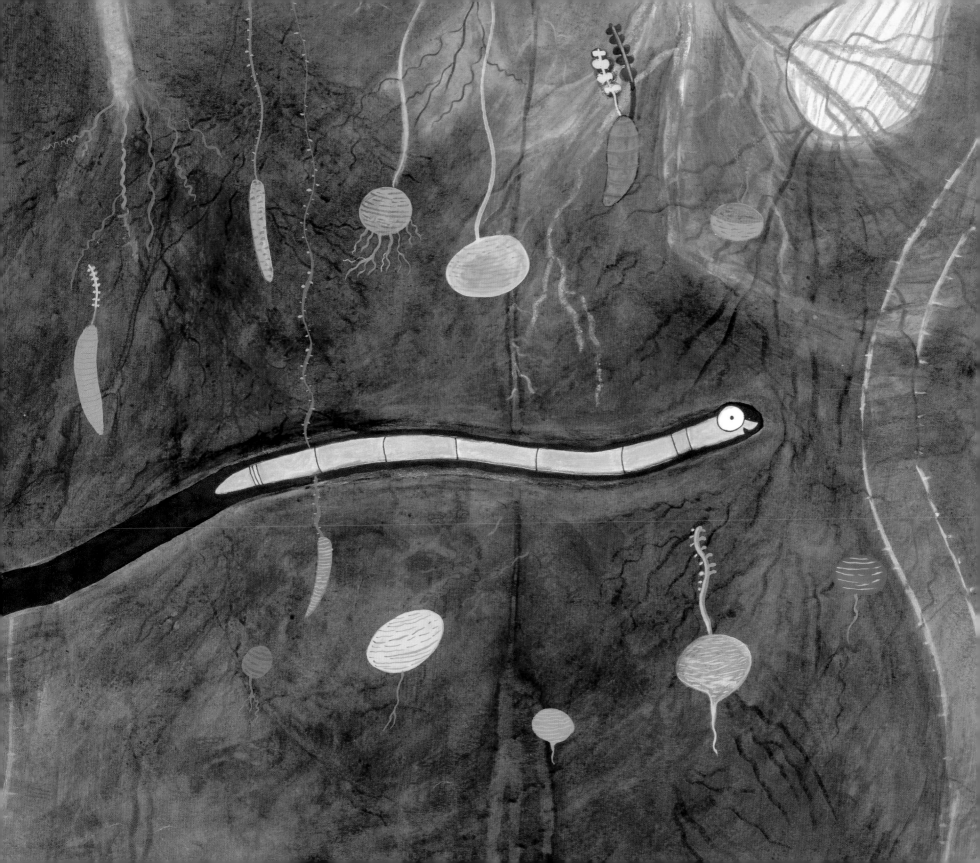

SNAIL

Three friends hid behind a rock.

Finally, the picnic people went home.

"What a mess," said Ladybug.

"Look at this trash," said Butterfly.

"I'll take care of it," said Snail.

She pushed the cup, the spoon, and the napkin

to the creek bank.

"You're a saint," said Ladybug.

"A real gem," said Butterfly.

Snail tinkered around a bit.

Then she pushed her new boat into the creek.

"No. I'm just a sail-snail.

And you two would make a great crew."

The friends hopped in the boat and

set sail together.

Litter bug

LIGHTNING BUG

Lightning Bug loved playing games:

tag,

kickball,

duck, duck, goose.

He never, ever won at

hide-and-go-seek,

but he was the all-time champion of

follow-the-leader.

THE GARDEN, AGAIN

The garden was old,

with a tumbledown wall

and a one-wheeled barrow.

But it wasn't forgotten

anymore

because they all called it

Home.

For Mom and Dad.
Thank you for a wonderful childhood, all of your love,
and that very special place called Home.
L. M.

For Max, with love x
G. M.

Text copyright © 2016 by Lisa Moser
Illustrations copyright © 2016 by Gwen Millward

First edition 2016

Library of Congress Catalog Card Number 2015937120
ISBN 978-0-7636-6534-0

15 16 17 18 19 20 LEO 10 9 8 7 6 5 4 3 2 1

Printed in Heshan, Guangdong, China

This book was typeset in Golden Cockerel.
The illustrations were done in ink, watercolor, and pencil.

Candlewick Press
99 Dover Street
Somerville, Massachusetts 02144

visit us at www.candlewick.com